TWELVE **12** WAYS

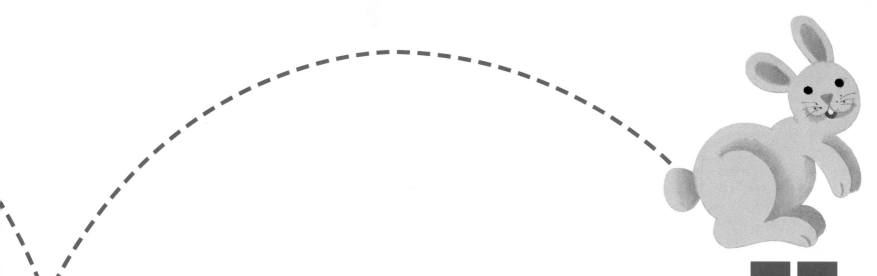

TO GET TO ELEVEN **11**

**Simon & Schuster
Books For Young Readers**

Published by Simon & Schuster

New York
London
Toronto
Sydney
Tokyo
Singapore

12 WAYS TO GET TO 11

Written
by
**EVE
MERRIAM**
•
Illustrated
by
**BERNIE
KARLIN**

1234567

The publisher deeply regrets the deaths of Eve Merriam and Bernie Karlin as this book was being prepared for publication.

SIMON & SCHUSTER BOOKS FOR YOUNG READERS
Simon & Schuster Building, Rockefeller Center
1230 Avenue of the Americas, New York, New York 10020.

Text copyright © 1993 by Eve Merriam.
Illustrations copyright © 1993 by Bernie Karlin.
All rights reserved including the right of reproduction
in whole or in part in any form.
SIMON & SCHUSTER BOOKS FOR YOUNG READERS
is a trademark of Simon & Schuster.

Designed by Bernie Karlin.
The text of this book is set in Avant Garde and Futura.
The illustrations were done in cut paper and colored pencil.
Manufactured in the United States of America.

10 9 8 7 6 5 4 3

Library of Congress Cataloging-in-Publication Data
Merriam, Eve. Twelve ways to get to eleven
by Eve Merriam: Illustrated by Bernie Karlin.
Summary: Uses ordinary experiences to present twelve combinations of numbers
that add up to eleven. Example: At the circus, six peanut shells and five pieces
of popcorn. 1 Addition—Juvenile literature. 2. Counting—Juvenile literature.
(1. Eleven (The number) 2. Addition. 3. Counting.)
I. Karlin. Bernie, ill. II. Title. III. Title: 12 ways to get to 11.
QA115.M47 1992   513.2 11—dc20
ISBN: 0-671-75544-7   91-25810 CIP

8 9 10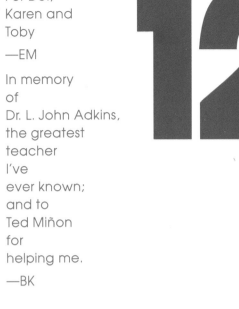

For Del,
Karen and
Toby
—EM

In memory
of
Dr. L. John Adkins,
the greatest
teacher
I've
ever known;
and to
Ted Miñon
for
helping me.
—BK

ONE, TWO,
THREE, FOUR,
FIVE, SIX,
SEVEN, EIGHT,
NINE, TEN,

TWELVE.

WHERE'S

ELEVEN?

Pick up
nine pinecones
from the forest floor
and two acorns.

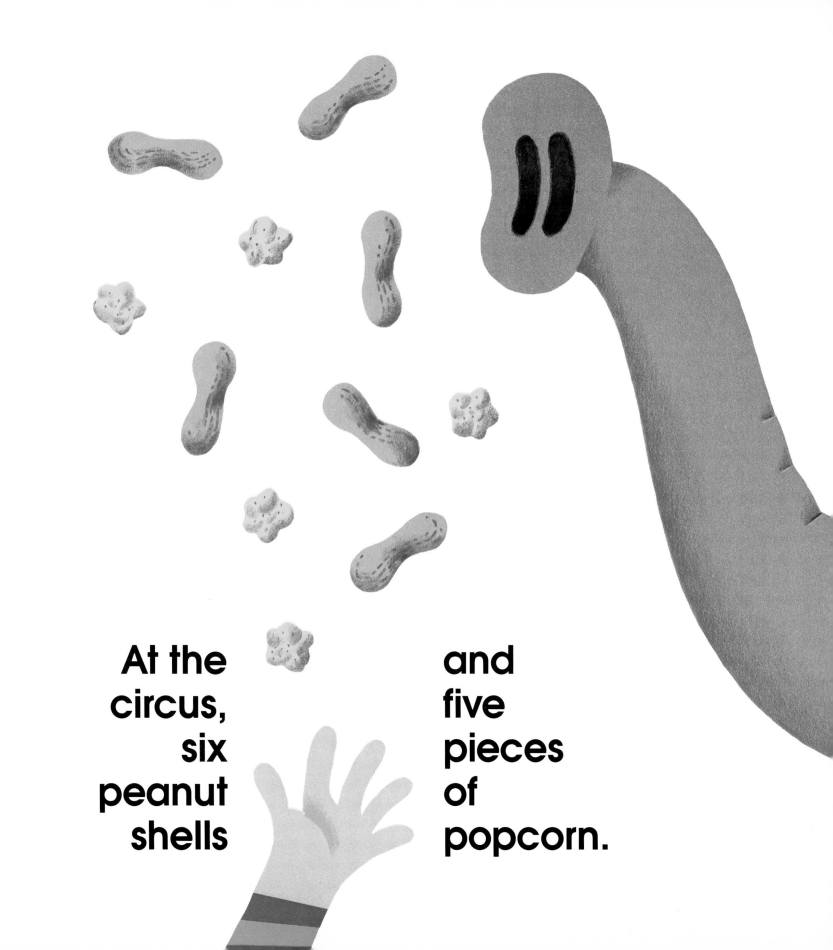

At the circus, six peanut shells and five pieces of popcorn.

Out of the magician's hat:
four banners,
five rabbits,
a pitcher of water,
and a
bouquet of flowers.

Go past four corners and two traffic lights,

then past the house with two chimneys

and the garage with two cars
and a bicycle.

Now look, you're at Eleventh Street.

Six bites,

a core,

a stem,

and
three
apple
seeds.

On the boat are two masts,
a big and a little sail,
four life preservers,
a flag, a ladder and
an anchor.

Three turtles sleeping,
two frogs swimming,
one lily pad,
and five dragonflies
darting on top of the pond.

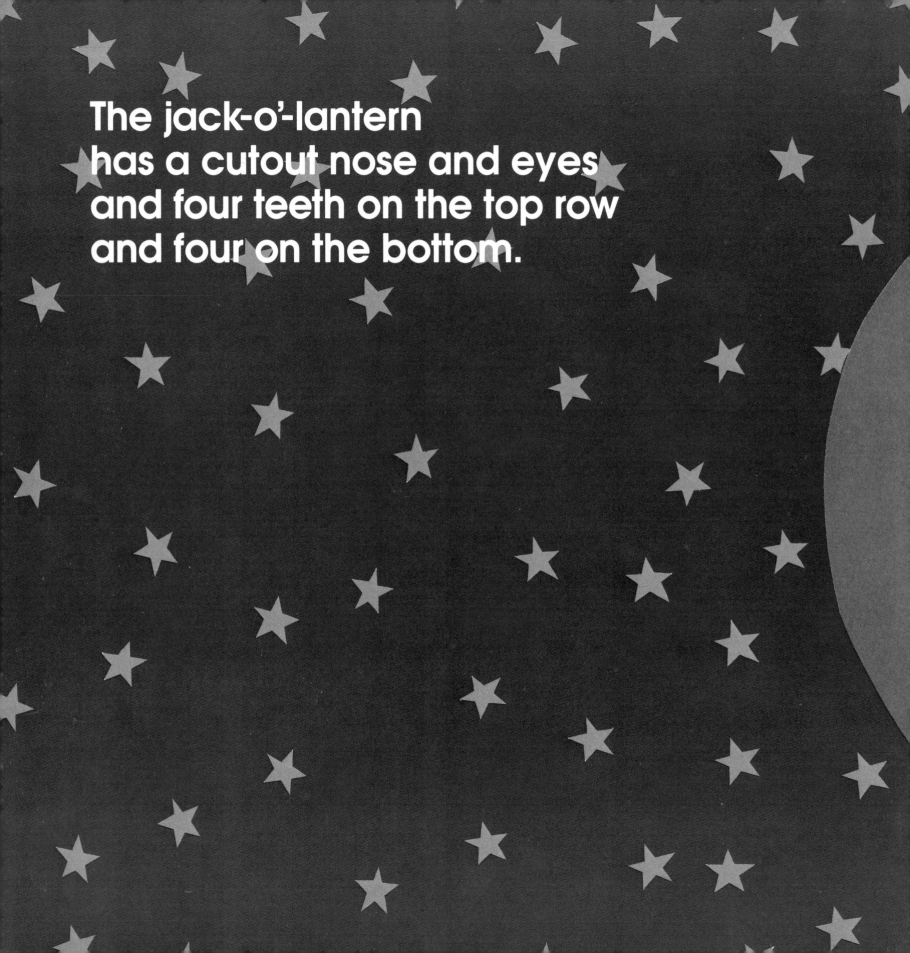

The jack-o'-lantern
has a cutout nose and eyes
and four teeth on the top row
and four on the bottom.

In the
mailbox:
seven letters,
two packages,
a mail-order
catalog,
and a
picture
postcard.

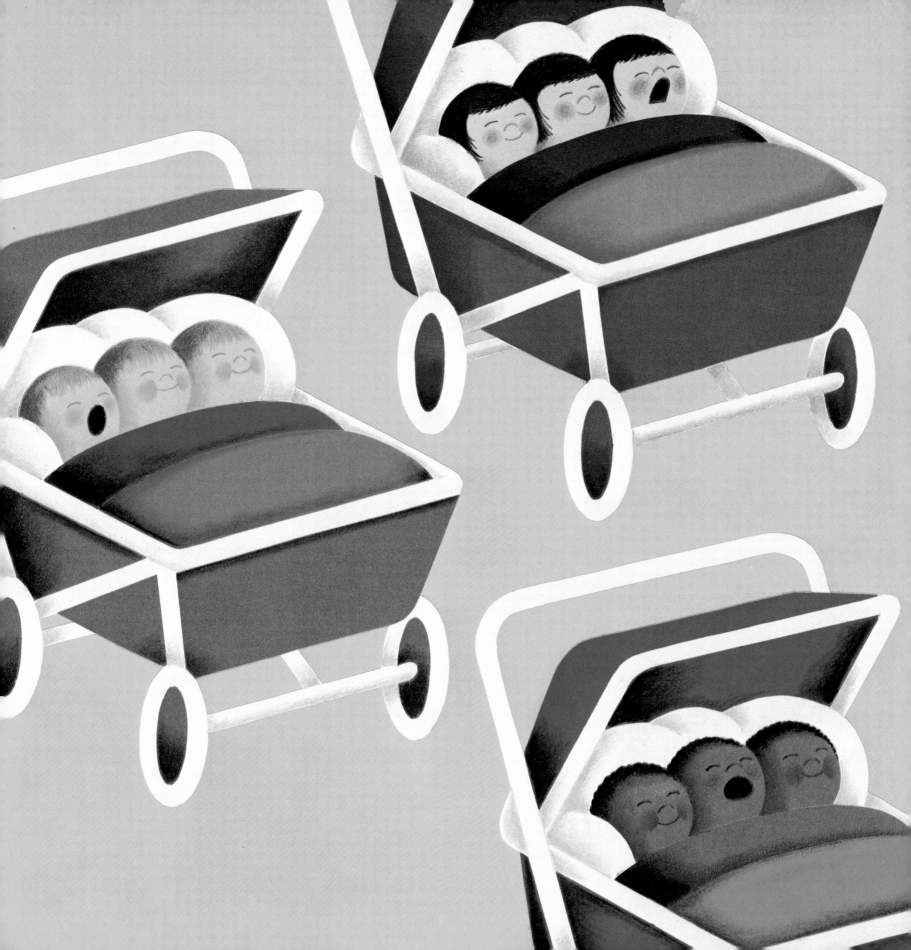

Three sets of triplets in baby carriages and a pair of twins in the stroller.

A sow
and ten
baby piglets.

In the hen yard:
five eggs,
three cracking open,
two beaks poking out,
and one just hatched.